DINOFOURS™

MY SEEDS WON'T GROW!

To Aunt Joyce
— S.M.

Go to www.scholastic.com for web site information on Scholastic authors and illustrators.

Text copyright © 2000 by Scholastic Inc.
Illustrations copyright © 2000 by Hans Wilhelm, Inc.
All rights reserved. Published by Scholastic Inc.
SCHOLASTIC, CARTWHEEL BOOKS and associated logos
are trademarks and/or registered trademarks of Scholastic Inc.

Library of Congress Cataloging-in-Publication Data
Metzger, Steve.
   Dinofours: my seeds won't grow! / by Steve Metzger; illustrated by Hans Wilhelm.
      p.   cm. — (Dinofours)
   "Cartwheel books."
   Summary: Upset that the plants he is growing are the smallest in the class, four-year-old dinosaur Brendan switches his name to another container but then regrets what he has done.
   ISBN 0-439-06329-9
   [1. Plants — Fiction. 2. Schools — Fiction. 3. Dinosaurs — Fiction.
   4. Honesty — Fiction.] I. Wilhelm, Hans, 1945- ill. II. Title.
   III. Title: My Seeds Won't Grow. IV. Series: Metzger, Steve. Dinofours.
   PZ7.M56775Dj   2000
      [E]—dc21   99-15530
                                                                                                      CIP

12 11 10 9 8 7 6 5 4 3 2 1   00 01 02 03 04
                                                                                                       24
Printed in the U.S.A.
First printing, March 2000

DINOFOURS™
MY SEEDS WON'T GROW!

by Steve Metzger
Illustrated by Hans Wilhelm

Cartwheel
·B·O·O·K·S·®

SCHOLASTIC INC.
New York   Toronto   London   Auckland   Sydney
Mexico City   New Delhi   Hong Kong

It was spring!

Mrs. Dee gathered the children around the science table.

"We're going to plant green bean seeds today," she said. "What do you think these seeds need to grow?"

"Dirt from the plant store," Danielle said.

"Yes," said Mrs. Dee. "It's also called soil. Anything else?"

"Water!" Joshua added.

"Sunshine, too!" said Tracy.

"My, my," said Mrs. Dee. "You know a lot about seeds. Now, how do you think they'll change?"

"Maybe they'll grow into a tall beanstalk, like the one in *Jack and the
Beanstalk*," Albert said. "That's a scary story with a giant."

"I really don't think that will happen," said Mrs. Dee. "Any other ideas?"

"These are green bean seeds," said Tara. "So they'll grow into green
bean plants."

"Let's plant the seeds now!" Brendan said excitedly. "I can't wait to see mine grow. They'll be the biggest in the whole class!"

"No, they won't!" said Tara.

"Yes, they will!" said Brendan. "You'll see."

"All right, children," said Mrs. Dee. "Let's begin."

Mrs. Dee gave each child three green bean seeds, some soil, a small container for planting, a spoon, and a measuring cup with water in it.

The children planted the seeds and watered them. Then, Mrs. Dee passed out craft sticks with their names on them to put in their containers.

"It's time to pick your next activity," Mrs. Dee announced. All the children left the table—except Brendan.

"I think I'll sit here and watch my seeds grow into plants," he said. Then, Brendan sang this song:

My seeds will grow and grow and grow—
So very big and tall.
They'll grow and grow until they are
The biggest plants of all!

"Brendan, it takes a while for seeds to grow," Mrs. Dee said.
"Okay," Brendan said as he walked away. "But I'll be back to check on them later."

For the next few days Brendan was the first child to arrive at school. He ran right to the windowsill where the seed containers were placed. It was always the same—nothing was growing.

"My seeds won't grow!" he said. "What's wrong?"

"There's nothing wrong," Mrs. Dee said. "You just need to be patient, that's all."

Brendan noticed that his soil was dry, so he added some water.

"Maybe tomorrow they'll grow," he said.

Two weeks passed and still no plants. That Friday afternoon, Mrs. Dee gathered the Dinofours to say good-bye for the weekend.

"I know everyone is hoping our green bean seeds will grow soon," she said.

"Especially me," said Brendan.

"Yes," said Mrs. Dee, "especially Brendan. Perhaps we'll see some changes on Monday morning."

"I hope so," said Brendan.

"And don't forget," Mrs. Dee said. "Monday is Danielle's birthday. We're going to have a class party to celebrate."

Everybody cheered. Then, Mrs. Dee dismissed the children to their parents, grandparents, and babysitters.

On Monday morning, Brendan was the first to arrive—as usual. He ran to the seed containers.

At first, Brendan was happy to see that all the children's seeds had sprouted. But when he compared his container with the others, his mood quickly changed.

My plants are the smallest, he said to himself. *And Joshua's are the biggest. How could that be?*

Making sure that no one was looking, Brendan switched his name stick with Joshua's. Now he had the tallest plants and Joshua had the smallest.

As the other children arrived, Brendan showed them how the seeds had grown.

"See, I told you I would have the tallest plants," he said.

Joshua saw that he had the smallest plants. Instead of getting upset, he shrugged his shoulders and walked away.

Later that day, the children gathered at the snack table for Danielle's birthday party.

"We're having blueberry muffins," Danielle said, pointing to the basket Mrs. Dee was holding. "My mommy and I baked them last night."

Mrs. Dee gave each child a muffin. Brendan noticed that the blueberries on his muffin made a face with a big smile.

"Look!" Brendan said to Tracy. "My muffin has a happy face. It's special."

Tracy looked at Brendan's muffin, then back at her own.

My muffin is so plain, she thought. *It's not special, like Brendan's.*

As the children turned their heads to sing "Happy Birthday" to Danielle, Tracy switched her muffin with Brendan's.

When Brendan saw what Tracy had done, he said, "You took my muffin. Give it back!"

"I'm Danielle's best friend," Tracy said. "I should have the special muffin!"

"No fair!" Brendan shouted. "That muffin is mine!"

Then, Brendan remembered how he had switched his name stick with Joshua's.

That wasn't fair either, he said to himself.

"Mrs. Dee," Brendan said. "I have something to tell you."

Mrs. Dee walked over to Brendan.

"This morning I saw that Joshua's plants were the biggest and mine were the smallest," he said. "I was sad, so I switched our names. I'm sorry."

"Brendan," Mrs. Dee replied. "I'm a little disappointed about what you did. But I'm very pleased to see how honest you are. Now let's talk to Joshua."

Brendan apologized to Joshua and sang this song to him:

When I switched our names today,
I hoped you wouldn't care.
But now I see
How bad it feels,
When things are so unfair.

"But now my plants are the smallest ones in the class," Brendan said. "I'm still sad about that."

"Maybe they'll catch up later," Joshua said.

And after a while, that's just what happened.